# The NUT STAYED SHUT

For Gem, Amos and Elias.

A TEMPLAR BOOK

First published in the UK in 2017 by Templar Publishing,
part of the Bonnier Publishing Group,
The Plaza, 535 King's Road, London, SW10 0SZ
www.templarco.co.uk
www.bonnierpublishing.com

1 3 5 7 9 10 8 6 4 2

ISBN 978-1-78370-693-8

Designed by Olivia Cook
Edited by Katie Haworth

Printed in China

# The NUT STAYED SHUT

Mike Henson

t

templar publishing

Of all the nut crackers in the world,
Rodney is the best.

So have a look,
three nuts to crack –
an easy-peasy test.

But what was this?

Rodney was oddly perplexed.
A nut he couldn't crack?

NONSENSE!

So he popped to the shed
for a hammer.

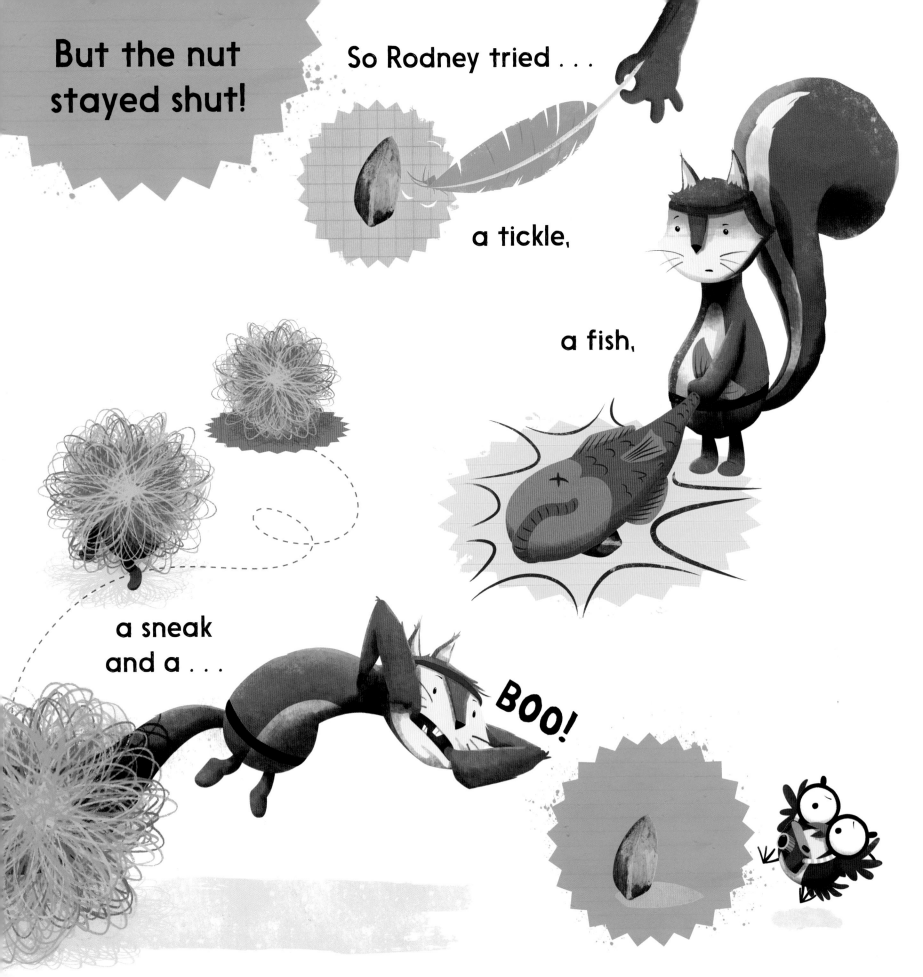

A chainsaw,

a door,

some rhinoceros poo.

But the nut stayed shut.

Maybe what he needed was something bigger . . .

. . . like an elephant,

or a digger.

But the nut stayed shut.

He tried a tree,

he tried a key,

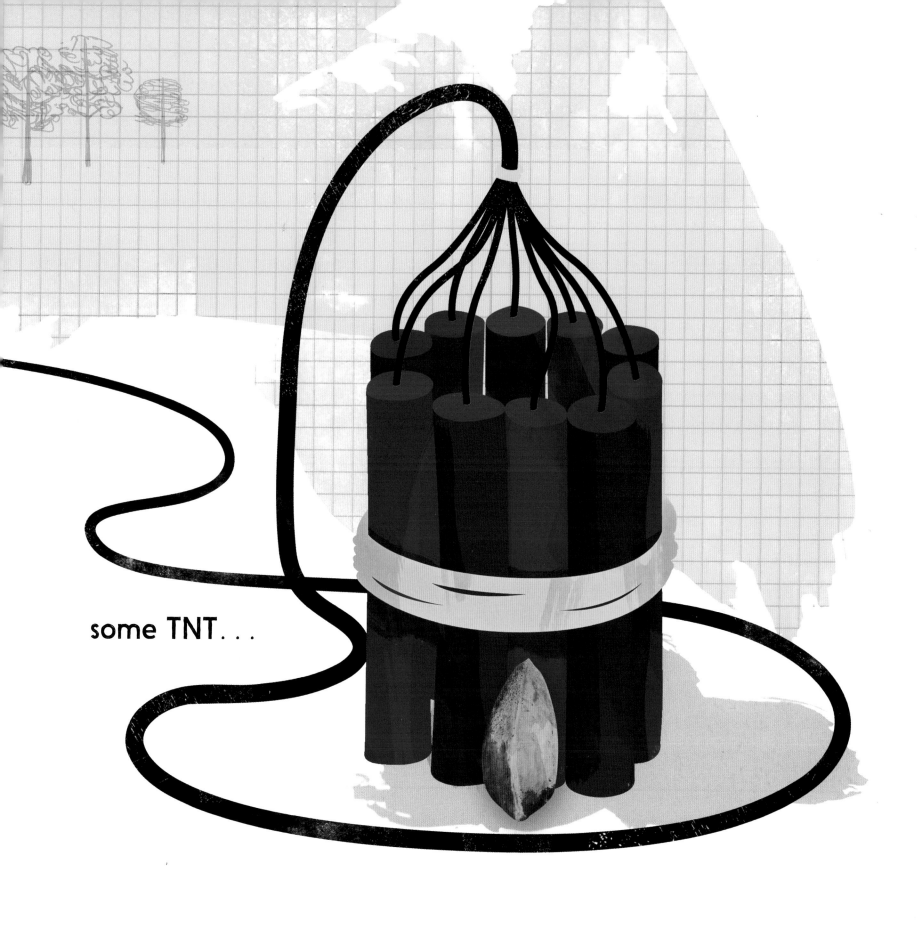

some TNT...

But the nut stayed shut.

It just wouldn't open up.

AAHHHHHHHHH

Don't walk away – it's not too late!
To crack some nuts, you have to . . .

. . . wait.

# More picture books from Templar:

ISBN: 978-1-78370-381-4 (Hardback)
978-1-78370-574-0 (Paperback)

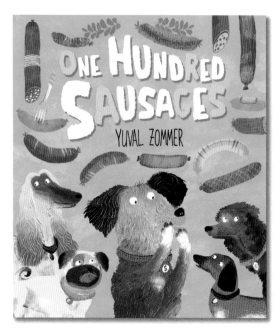

ISBN: 978-1-78370-575-7 (Hardback)
978-1-78370-576-4 (Paperback)

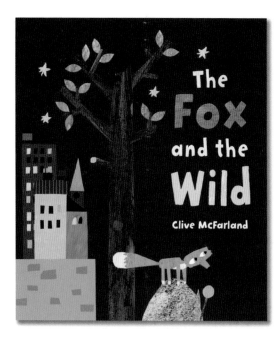

ISBN: 978-1-78370-386-9 (Hardback)
978-1-78370-387-6 (Paperback)

ISBN: 978-1-78370-238-1 (Hardback)
978-1-78370-239-8 (Paperback)